Cat Club

Abyssinians

by Cameron L. Woodson

Bullfrog Books

Ideas for Parents and Teachers

Bullfrog Books let children practice reading informational text at the earliest reading levels. Repetition, familiar words, and photo labels support early readers.

Before Reading

- Discuss the cover photo. What does it tell them?
- Look at the picture glossary together. Read and discuss the words.

Read the Book

- "Walk" through the book and look at the photos. Let the child ask questions. Point out the photo labels.
- Read the book to the child, or have him or her read independently.

After Reading

- Prompt the child to think more. Ask: Abyssinians can be shy around new people. Can you think of other animals that can be shy?

Bullfrog Books are published by Jump!
5357 Penn Avenue South
Minneapolis, MN 55419
www.jumplibrary.com

Library of Congress Cataloging-in-Publication Data

Names: Woodson, Cameron L., 1994– author.
Title: Abyssinians / Cameron L. Woodson.
Description: Minneapolis: Jump!, Inc., [2021]
Series: Cat club | Includes index.
Audience: Ages 5–8 | Audience: Grades K–1
Identifiers: LCCN 2019048799 (print)
LCCN 2019048800 (ebook)
ISBN 9781645274438 (hardcover)
ISBN 9781645274445 (ebook)
Subjects: LCSH: Abyssinian cat—Juvenile literature.
Classification: LCC SF449.A28 W66 2021 (print)
LCC SF449.A28 (ebook)
DDC 636.8/26—dc23
LC record available at https://lccn.loc.gov/2019048799
LC ebook record available at
https://lccn.loc.gov/2019048800

Editors: Jenna Gleisner and Susanne Bushman
Designer: Jenna Casura

Photo Credits: Asichka/Shutterstock, cover; fotojagodka/iStock, 1; Seregraff/Shutterstock, 3; Mariana Mikhailova/iStock, 4; Oks88/iStock, 5; Ekaterina_Polischuk/iStock, 6–7; nelik/iStock, 8–9 (foreground); cmannphoto/iStock, 8–9 (background); Candy_Vandy/iStock, 10; ilietus/iStock, 11, 22tr; Natalia Tretiakova/Shutterstock, 12–13 (cat on perch), 22br; Africa Studio/Shutterstock, 12–13 (room), 22br; MyImages - Micha/Shutterstock, 14l, 22tl; Anton Akhmatov/Shutterstock, 14r, 22tl; S_zt/Shutterstock, 15; GCapture/Shutterstock, 16–17; Yulia Vybornyh/Shutterstock, 18–19, 22bl; fotogeng/Shutterstock, 20–21; Borkin Vadim/Shutterstock, 22; Sergey Taran/Dreamstime, 24.

Printed in the United States of America at Corporate Graphics in North Mankato, Minnesota.

Table of Contents

Curious Cats 4
An Abyssinian Up Close 22
Picture Glossary 23
Index 24
To Learn More 24

Curious Cats

This is an Abyssinian!

We call it an Aby.

Abys have big ears!

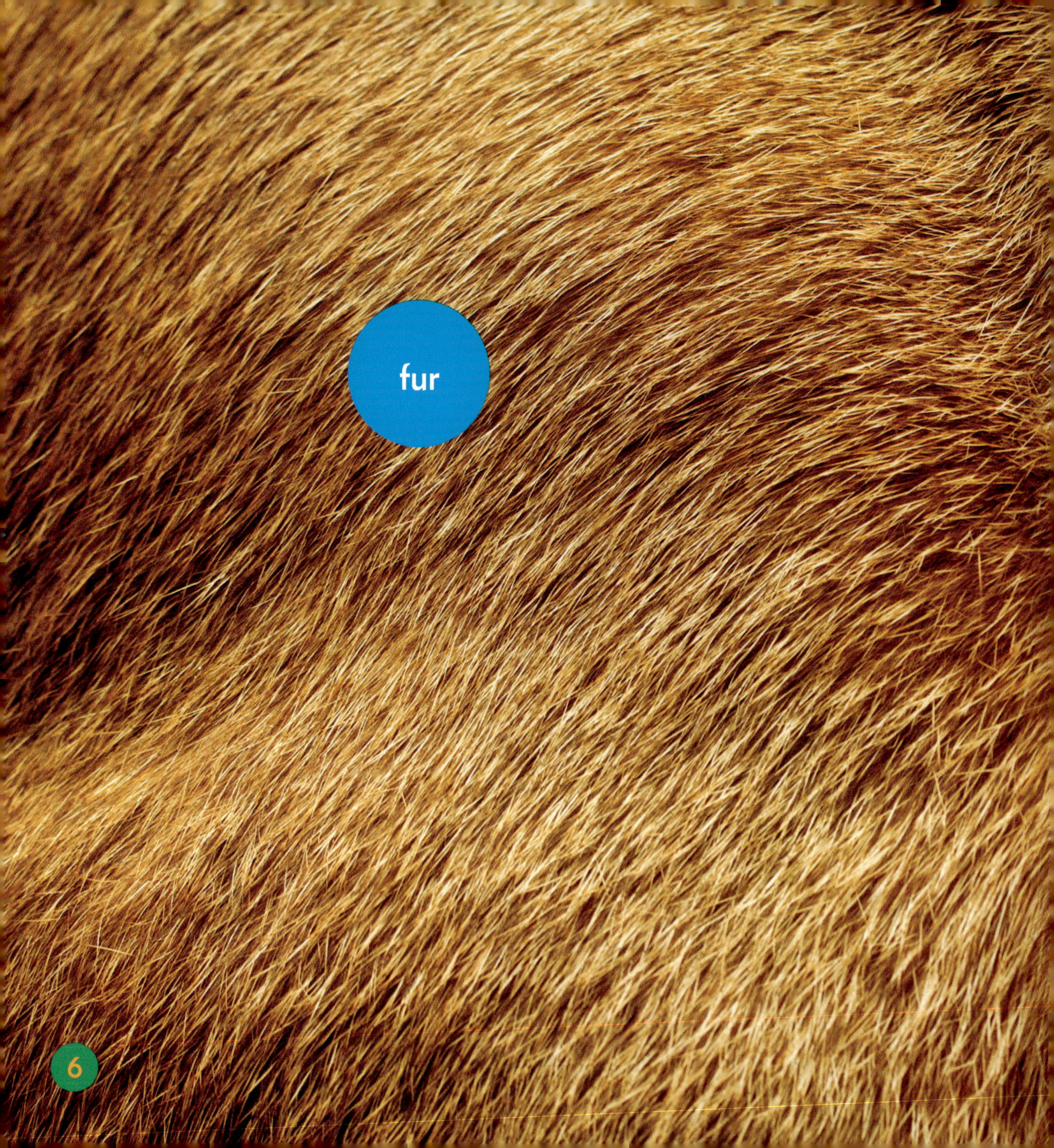
fur

They have short fur.
It is reddish brown.
Cool!

Fur on the tail
is different.

The tip is black!

This Aby's eyes are green.

Others are hazel or gold.

perch

Abys like to be up high.

This one loves its perch.

These cats love to play.
They are curious.
They are smart, too.

They take things. Why?

They want to learn about them.

Some Abys are shy.

A new friend comes over.

This Aby hides.

But she loves her owner!

Would you like an Aby?

An Abyssinian Up Close

An Abyssinian has long, thin legs and large ears. Its fur is short. Look at its other body parts!

Picture Glossary

curious
Eager to know or learn about something.

hazel
A green-brown color.

owner
Someone who owns a pet.

perch
A raised place where a cat can sit.

Index

curious 14
ears 5
eyes 10
fur 7, 8
hides 16
learn 15
owner 19
perch 13
play 14
shy 16
smart 14
tail 8

To Learn More

Finding more information is as easy as 1, 2, 3.

1. Go to www.factsurfer.com
2. Enter "Abyssinians" into the search box.
3. Click the "Surf" button to see a list of websites.